For Poppy Isabella McGrath. J.W.

For Llewelyn Thomas Seddon Oliver. A.R.

Also by Jeanne Willis and Adrian Reynolds:

I'm Sure I Saw a Dinosaur
That's Not Funny!
Upside Down Babies

First American edition published in 2015 by Andersen Press USA, an imprint of Andersen Press Ltd.

www.andersenpressusa.com

First published in Great Britain in 2015 by Andersen Press Ltd.,

20 Vauxhall Bridge Road, London SW1V 2SA.

Published in Australia by Random House Australia Pty.,

Level 3, 100 Pacific Highway, North Sydney, NSW 2060.

Text copyright © Jeanne Willis, 2015.

Illustration copyright © Adrian Reynolds, 2015

Distributed in the United States and Canada by

Lerner Publishing Group, Inc.

241 First Avenue North

Minneapolis, MN 55401 USA

For reading levels and more information, look up this title at www.lernerbooks.com.

Color separated in Switzerland by Photolitho AG, Zürich.

Printed and bound in Malaysia by Tien Wah Press.

Library of Congress Cataloging-in-Publication data available.

ISBN: 978-1-4677-6316-5

eBook ISBN: 978-1-4677-6320-2

1 – TWP – 07/01/14

ELEPHANTS CAN'T JUMP!

JEANNE WILLIS
ADRIAN REYNOLDS

ANDERSEN PRESS USA

Even giraffes can jump . . .

. . . but elephants can't.
"Why not?" asked Elephant.

"It's just the way we're made," said his mother.
"Something to do with our knees," said his father.
"Among other things," said his auntie.

**But Elephant wouldn't give up.
"If I ran fast enough, I could jump
over that log," he thought.**

So he ran his very fastest and . . .

... went
tail over
trunk.

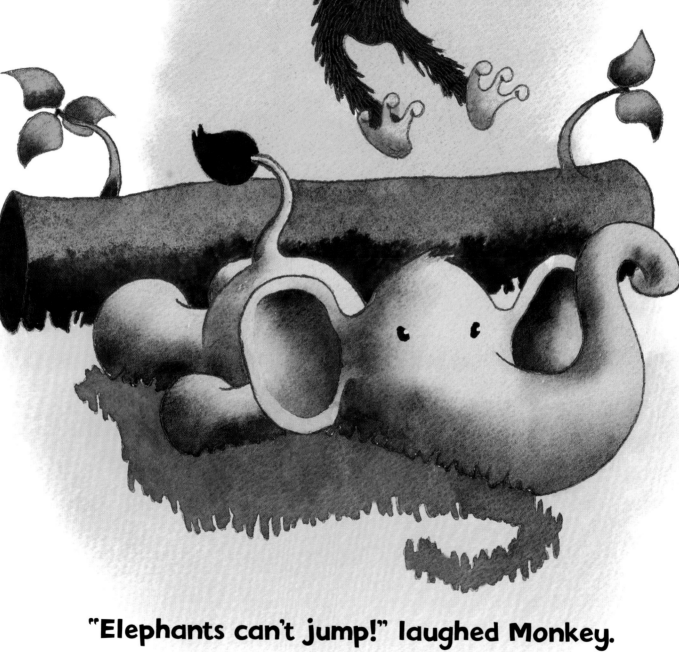

"Elephants can't jump!" laughed Monkey.
"If I had something to bounce off, I could,"
thought Elephant.

So he found something bouncy.

But no matter how hard he tried to jump up . . .

. . . he stayed down.

**"Elephants can't jump!" laughed Lion.
"Maybe I could jump off something high,"
thought Elephant.**

So he climbed to the top of a hill and he went,
"Ready, steady . . . **whoops!**"

"Elephants can't jump!" laughed Giraffe.

"Perhaps I could if I wasn't so heavy," thought Elephant.
So he had no dinner for **five** whole days.
Then he tried again. One, two, **three, jump** ...

"Elephants can't jump!" all the animals laughed.

Elephant gave up.
He ate and ate, and got
bigger and **bigger**.

But he still felt very small **on the inside.**

Elephant went up a mountain to sulk.

But when he looked down, he saw a boy
who had fallen onto a rock below.

"Help!" cried the boy.

"Jump down and save me!"

"Elephants can't jump. I'll save you," said Monkey. Monkey jumped, but the boy was too heavy to lift and he was too scared to let go of Monkey.

"I'll jump down and save you," said Lion.
But the boy clung to Monkey, and when Monkey
climbed onto Lion, Lion couldn't jump back.

"Help!" they cried.

"I'll save you!" cried Giraffe, jumping down.
"Grab my neck, boy!"
But the boy was too scared. He clung to Monkey,
Monkey clung to Lion, and Lion clung to Giraffe.

"Help, we're going to fall!" they cried.
"We can't save you!"

Suddenly, Elephant found his own
strength. He reached out with his long,
strong trunk and wrapped it around
Giraffe. Giraffe clung to Lion. Monkey
clung to the boy. Elephant pulled with
all his mighty **might** and . . .

. . . **Up** came **Giraffe!**

Up came **Lion!**

Up came **Monkey!**

Up came **the boy!**

They were so happy to be saved that
they jumped **UP** and **down**.

Elephant couldn't. But that didn't matter because he had done something no other animal could do. Not even Lion or Monkey or Giraffe.

Elephant was a **hero!**

"Hooray for Elephant!" everyone cheered.

And although Elephant kept his feet firmly on the ground . . .

. . . his heart **jumped** for **joy!**